OLIVER PIG
AT
SCHOOL

Jean Van Leeuwen

PICTURES BY

ANN SCHWENINGER

DIAL BOOKS FOR YOUNG READERS

NEW YORK

Published by Dial Books for Young Readers
A Division of Penguin Books USA Inc.
375 Hudson Street
New York, New York 10014

Printed in Hong Kong by South China Printing Company (1988) Limited

The Dial Easy-to-Read logo is a registered trademark of
Dial Books for Young Readers, A Division of
Penguin Books USA Inc., ® TM 1,162,718.

Library of Congress Cataloging in Publication Data
Van Leeuwen, Jean. Oliver Pig at school
by Jean Van Leeuwen; pictures by Ann Schweninger.
p. cm.
Summary: During Oliver Pig's first day at school,
he builds with blocks, plays with his toy
dinosaur, and makes a new friend.
ISBN 0-8037-0812-2.—ISBN 0-8037-0813-0 (lib. bdg.)
[1. Schools—Fiction. 2. Pigs—Fiction.]
I. Schweninger, Ann, ill. II. Title.
PZ7.V32730mn 1990 [E]—dc20 89-25607 CIP AC

E
3 5 7 9 10 8 6 4 2

The full-color artwork was prepared using carbon pencil,
colored pencils, and watercolor washes. It was then scanner-separated
and reproduced as red, blue, yellow, and black halftones.

Reading Level 2.0

For David, who didn't cry
on his first day

J.V. L.

For Toby Sherry

A.S.

CONTENTS

THE FIRST DAY

"Wake up, Oliver," said Mother.

"Do you remember what day it is?"

"Yes!" said Oliver.

This was the day he'd been waiting for,

the first day of school.

Oliver jumped out of bed.

He put on his new striped shirt

and his new red overalls.

"How do I look?" he asked.

"All grown up," said Mother.

"And handsome."

There were pancakes for breakfast.

They were Oliver's favorite.

But it was hard to sit still to eat.

Oliver took three bites.

"Is it time for the school bus yet?"

he asked.

"Almost," said Father.

Oliver walked around the house,
saying good-bye to his things.
"Good-bye, bike," he said.
"Good-bye, trucks and Tiger
and all you dinosaurs."
He picked up his littlest dinosaur
and put him in his pocket.

"You can go to school with me,"
he said.

Mother and Father and Amanda
walked Oliver to the bus stop.

Oliver looked down the road.
There was the school bus,
big and yellow and noisy.

"Good-bye, Amanda," said Oliver.

"Too bad you're too little

to go to school. But don't worry,

I'll play with you when I come home.

Good-bye, Mother and Father."

Mother and Father kissed Oliver.

"Have fun at school," said Father.

Oliver climbed up the tall steps
and found a seat by the window.

"Good-bye, Oliver!"

Mother and Father and Amanda

were waving to him.

"Good-bye!" He waved back.

Then the bus started moving.

And they were gone.

Oliver was all alone.

Suddenly his eyes felt funny,

like they wanted to cry.

What was the matter with them?

Oliver looked around.

Everyone on the school bus looked big.

They were talking and laughing.

But no one talked and laughed with him.

Maybe no one would talk to him all day.

Suddenly his stomach felt funny,

like something was jumping

up and down inside of it.

Oliver sat very still in his seat

until the school bus stopped.

Everyone started to get off.

Oliver did not want to get off.

He wanted to go home.

He reached into his pocket,

and there was his little dinosaur.

Oliver squeezed him tight.

Slowly he climbed down the tall steps.

Waiting at the bottom was his teacher.

"I am Miss Jessie Pig," she said.

"I am Oliver," said Oliver.

She looked just like Grandmother.

"What do you like to do most, Oliver?"

asked Miss Jessie Pig.

"Build with blocks and read books,"

said Oliver.

"In my room we have giant blocks,"

she said. "And lots of books.

Would you like to come and see?"

"Yes," said Oliver.

With one hand holding hers

and the other holding his dinosaur,

Oliver walked down the hall

to Miss Jessie Pig's room.

NECKLACES

Miss Jessie Pig's room

was full of toys,

even more than Oliver had at home.

And everyone there was just his size.

Oliver played trucks with James.

He made a road in the sandbox
with Alexander.

And he built a giant castle
out of giant blocks with Rosie.

Then Miss Jessie Pig said,
"Now it is art time."
On a table she put bowls
of buttons and beads and noodles
and pink Puff-Doodles cereal.
"Today we will make necklaces,"
she said.

Oliver put a blue button on his string.

Then he put on three Puff-Doodles.

He looked at his necklace.

He smelled it.

It smelled like breakfast.

Suddenly Oliver was very hungry.

He took off the three Puff-Doodles
and ate them.

"Look at my necklace," said Victoria.

"It is all pink."

Oliver put a pink bead on his string
and four more Puff-Doodles.

Then he remembered that
he'd only had three bites of pancake
for breakfast.

He ate the four Puff-Doodles too.

"Look at my necklace," said Victoria.

"It's all finished.

May I make a bracelet too?"

"Certainly," said Miss Jessie Pig.

Oliver wasn't finished.

He had barely started.

He put on three noodles,

five Puff-Doodles, a silver button,

and six more noodles.

Now it looked more like a necklace.

Then he took off the noodles

and Puff-Doodles.

The noodles were crunchy,

but Oliver didn't care.

He was still hungry.

"Look at my bracelet," said Victoria.

"It's all purple."

"Mine is silver and gold," said Rosie.

"I made a noodle Puff-Doodle necklace,"

said James.

Everyone was wearing their necklaces.

"Oliver," said Miss Jessie Pig.

"Where is your necklace?"

Oliver looked down at his string

with only a blue button, a pink bead,

and a silver button on the end.

"I didn't make a necklace," he said.

"I made a ring."

BAD BERNARD

"Now it is story time,"

said Miss Jessie Pig.

She read to them a book

about a bad monkey.

Oliver sat next to Bernard.

Bernard kept kicking him.

"Stop that," whispered Oliver.

Bernard stopped kicking.

Instead he poked Oliver.

"Stop that!" said Oliver out loud.

Miss Jessie Pig stopped reading.

"Oliver, sit next to Rosie," she said.

"Bernard, you may sit next to James."

After story time was snack time.

Miss Jessie Pig put a plate of cookies

in the middle of the table.

Oliver wasn't hungry anymore.

But then he saw that they were

oatmeal cookies, his favorite.

And there was only one left.

He reached for it.

So did Bernard.

"It's mine!" said Oliver.

"No, mine!" said Bernard.

They both pulled on the cookie.

Juice spilled all over the table.

"Oliver! Bernard!"

said Miss Jessie Pig.

"It looks as if you two

will be my cleanup helpers today."

Oliver did not like Bernard.

He was bad,

just like the monkey in the story.

At playtime in the playground

he crashed cars with Oliver.

"Ka-pow!"

He smashed into Alexander

coming down the slide.

"Ka-pooey!"

Then it was rest time.

Oliver was glad. He needed a rest.

He unrolled a rug and lay down.

The room was very quiet.

Oliver took his dinosaur for a walk

through the jungle of his rug.

Suddenly they came face-to-face

with another dinosaur.

Oliver looked up.

There, on the next rug, was Bernard.

"What is your dinosaur's name?"

whispered Bernard.

"Stegosaurus," whispered Oliver.

"What's yours?"

"Brontosaurus," said Bernard.

Together, Oliver's dinosaur
and Bernard's dinosaur climbed up
the mountain of Bernard's leg.

"Sssshh!" said Miss Jessie Pig.

"Remember, Oliver and Bernard,
rest time is quiet time."

Oliver and Bernard

put their dinosaurs to sleep

in the cave under Oliver's rug.

"*Sssshh!*" they said.

Then, together,

they closed their eyes to rest.

GOING HOME

"And now," said Miss Jessie Pig,

"I have a surprise for you."

The surprise was a big red box.

"Rosie, will you open it?" she said.

Inside the box were drums

and whistles and rattles

and jingle bells and kazoos.

"This is my music box,"

said Miss Jessie Pig.

"Would anyone like

to make a little music?"

Rosie and Bernard played drums.

Victoria played jingle bells.

Oliver played a kazoo.

And everyone sang.

They sang songs about spiders

and monkeys and smiling faces.

"That was fun," said Oliver.

"Can we do it again?"

"Tomorrow," said Miss Jessie Pig.

"Tomorrow we will paint pictures

and write our ABC's

and I will read you a dinosaur book.

But now do you know what time it is?"

"Playtime again?" guessed Bernard.

"No," she said. "It is going-home time."

"Already?" said Oliver.

He helped clean up

the blocks and books and trucks.

Then everyone put on their necklaces.

Oliver put on his ring.

And they all walked outside
to the school bus.
Oliver climbed up the tall steps
and found a seat next to Bernard.

All the way home
they laughed and talked
and took their dinosaurs climbing
up the slippery ice of the bus window.

Then the bus stopped at Oliver's corner.

"Good-bye," said Oliver.

"See you tomorrow," said Bernard.

"Don't forget your dinosaur."

Oliver climbed down the tall steps.

And there were Mother and Father

and Amanda, waiting for him.

Mother and Father hugged him.

"How was it?" Mother asked.

"I didn't cry," said Oliver.

"And my teacher is nice

and I have a new friend

and I made a ring at art time

and tomorrow we get to read

a book about dinosaurs."

"It sounds like you had fun at school,"
said Father.

"Yes," said Oliver.

"School is fun."